PUFFIN BOOKS

Lightning Lucy

Jeremy Strong once worked in a bakery, putting the jam into three thousand doughnuts every night. Now he puts the jam in stories instead, which he finds much more exciting. At the age of three he fell out of a first floor bedroom window and landed on his head. His mother says that this damaged him for the rest of his life and refuses to take any responsibility. He loves writing stories because he says it is 'the only time you alone have complete control and can make anything happen'.' His ambition is to make you laugh (or at least snuffle). Jeremy Strong lives in Kent with his family, which includes a small but very noticeable cat called Machiavelli.

Other books by Jeremy Strong

MY DAD'S GOT AN ALLIGATOR!
MY GRANNY'S GREAT ESCAPE
THE DESPERATE ADVENTURES OF SIR RUPERT AND ROSIE GUSSET
FATBAG: THE DEMON VACUUM CLEANER
THE HUNDRED MILE-AN-HOUR DOG
THE INDOOR PIRATES

THERE'S A PHARAOH IN OUR BATH
THERE'S A VIKING IN MY BED
VIKING IN TROUBLE

THE KARATE PRINCESS
THE KARATE PRINCESS AND THE CUT-THROAT ROBBERS
THE KARATE PRINCESS TO THE RESCUE
THE KARATE PRINCESS AND THE LAST GRIFFIN

Jeremy Strong

Lightning Lucy

Illustrated by Toni Goffe

PUFFIN BOOKS

PUFFIN BOOKS

Published by the Penguin Group
Penguin Books Ltd, 27 Wrights Lane, London W8 5TZ, England
Penguin Books USA Inc., 375 Hudson Street, New York, New York 10014, USA
Penguin Books Australia Ltd, Ringwood, Victoria, Australia
Penguin Books Canada Ltd, 10 Alcorn Avenue, Toronto, Ontario, Canada M4V 3B2
Penguin Books (NZ) Ltd, 182–190 Wairau Road, Auckland 10, New Zealand

Penguin Books Ltd, Registered Offices: Harmondsworth, Middlesex, England

First published by A & C Black 1982
Published in Puffin Books 1993
5 7 9 10 8 6 4

Filmset in Monophoto Plantin

Made and printed in England by Clays Ltd, St Ives plc

British Library Cataloguing in Publication Data
A CIP catalogue record for this book is available from the British Library

ISBN 0–140–36145–6

1

Can Four Year Olds Fly?

Nobody thought there was anything special about Lucy until she fell into the garden pond. Lucy was just four at the time. Before that happened, Lucy's mum, Mrs King, had thought that Lucy was just a nuisance and messy and noisy – but not extra-special. Mr King thought Lucy was sweet, pretty and a little imp – but not extra-special. Lucy's two year old brother, Nicholas, didn't think about his sister at all and neither did the family cat, Flop.

But that was before Lucy fell into the pond. It wasn't a very large pond, but it was right in the middle of the garden. It had a rockery and clumps of stunted flowers around it. Mrs King kept trying to grow pretty little rock-plants but Lucy spent so much time mountaineering on the rockery that it didn't look like anything much at all. The pond wasn't very deep, but it was deeper than Lucy was tall. There were real fish in it, and frogs, and great floating, weedy leaves that had snails underneath them.

This particular day was warm and sunny. There wasn't a cloud in sight and Lucy had spent most of the morning running round the garden doing helpful things, like pulling up the flowers and shoving them in the pond because she thought they needed water.

A small plane flew overhead and began to twist and dive and zoom up in the air and roll over. Lucy was fascinated. She stood in the sunshine and watched the plane go through all its acrobatics. It was just as if the pilot was putting on a display especially for Lucy. The plane came tumbling out of the sky, rolling over and over directly above her. She took a couple of steps back to keep the plane in view, and with the second step there was a tremendous splash and she disappeared into the pond.

Water streamed over the sides and dribbled down the rockery. All that could be seen of Lucy was a pair of dirty white socks and muddy sandals sticking out of the water, kicking furiously. Mr and Mrs King, who had been sunbathing, dashed towards the pond to haul their drowning daughter out.

Suddenly a fountain of water exploded upwards, soaking them both. Lucy rocketed out of the pond, her arms stretched out above her head, trailing long streamers of green weed. She zoomed straight up into the topmost branches of the apple tree, clasped her arms round a branch and began to howl dismally.

Mr King stared up at his daughter, frozen with shock. Mrs King pinched herself hard, to make sure that she hadn't been seeing things. Lucy wailed from the top of the apple tree. Her father swallowed and gulped.

'I'll get a ladder,' he said, and hurried over to

the garden shed. He put the ladder against the tree, climbed up and carefully carried Lucy down. She was still crying. Mrs King took her inside to dry her off.

It was twenty minutes before Mr King had a chance to talk to his wife, because she was busy putting Lucy to bed.

'She was shocked, Harold,' said Mrs King.

'I'm not surprised. I was too. Didn't you see what I saw?'

'I don't know.' Mrs King wrung her hands. 'I don't know what I saw.'

'Surely you saw what I saw!' cried Mr King. 'Didn't you? Tell me what you saw first.' Mrs King bit her lip and stared anxiously at her husband.

'I just don't know, Harold. It all happened so quickly.'

'That's just it,' exclaimed Mr King. 'If it had happened slowly it would all make sense. You don't want to tell me what you saw because you can't believe it can you? Well, I'll tell you what I saw. There was a whoosh of water and our Lucy came flying out of that pond. Don't screw your eyes up like that Elsie, she was flying. Flying, and there were weeds trailing from her arms and legs.' Mr King had jumped up and was marching nervously round the room.

'She'd gone sort of red,' added Mrs King in a quiet murmur, as if she still could not believe it. 'There was a sort of red glow all round her.'

'Lucy wasn't red,' said Mr King. 'It was a glow all around her.' Mrs King nodded.

'And then,' continued Mr King in a matter-of-fact kind of voice, 'she flew up into the old apple tree and sat in the top branches and cried.'

'The glow went first,' said Mrs King. 'The glow faded as she landed in the tree.'

'There,' said Mr King. 'You saw exactly what I saw.' There was a long silence as the two worried parents stared at each other. Mrs King began to cry.

'I don't understand it,' she sobbed. 'Children can't fly, Harold. At least they shouldn't. I mean who taught her to fly? They don't teach flying at school nowadays, do they?'

Mr King sat down next to his wife and put a comforting arm round her. 'Perhaps we just dreamed it. Maybe it never happened at all. It could simply be that . . .'

'But we both saw it!' wailed Mrs King. 'Our Lucy, flying through the air!'

Mr King sighed. 'I'll telephone for the doctor.'

Mrs King gave a tearful smile and asked, 'Is he coming to see us, or Lucy?' Mr King laughed and patted his wife's shoulder.

'I don't think we're that mad. He ought to see Lucy. She could catch an awful cold from that ducking.'

By the time the doctor called, it was mid-afternoon. Mrs King had put young Nicholas in his cot for an afternoon sleep, but Lucy was wide awake and running about as if nothing had happened at all. Dad wouldn't let her play in the garden and that made Lucy angry.

'Why can't I?' she kept asking, tossing back her curls.

'Because you may fall in the pond again.'

'But I've never fallen in the pond!' protested Lucy. Mr King stared at her.

'Surely you remember falling in the pond?'

Lucy shook her head crossly. At that moment the doorbell rang and Mrs King let the doctor in. Doctor Evans was quite young. He was a good doctor with children and Lucy liked him.

'Hallo young Lucy,' he said. 'Have you got the measles again?' Lucy smiled and shook her head. The doctor turned to look at Mr and Mrs King.

'We're a bit worried about her,' began Mr King. 'I think you'd better go out and play Lucy, while we talk to the doctor.'

'Outside?' repeated Lucy.

'Yes, but keep away from the pond.' They

watched Lucy run out into the garden. Doctor Evans smiled as he watched her go.

'She seems to be in the best of health. I can't think what's worrying you about her.' He sat down in an armchair.

Mr King sat down on the sofa next to his wife. He grasped his hands firmly in his lap and looked straight at Doctor Evans.

'Can four year olds fly?' he asked. Doctor Evans blinked several times and raised his eyebrows with much surprise.

'I beg your pardon?' he said at last.

'We want to know if four year olds can fly,' repeated Mrs King, and she went on to tell the doctor the whole extraordinary story of Lucy and the pond.

Doctor Evans listened without saying a word. He just sat back in the armchair with his mouth dropping further and further open and his eyes getting rounder and rounder. His hands gripped the arms of his chair and when Mrs King had finished he said quietly, 'Could I have a cup of tea, Mrs King?' He gave a funny sort of laugh and scratched his head rapidly. The poor doctor seemed very confused.

'It's an odd story,' he said at last. 'I'm sure there must be a good explanation for it.' He tried to smile.

'Yes?' asked Mr King, waiting for the good explanation.

'I'm trying to think of one,' said Doctor Evans desperately, and he gave that funny, nervous laugh again. Mrs King broke the long silence that followed when she brought in the tea. The doctor sipped at his cup gratefully.

'Let's have a look at Lucy, then,' he suggested. 'She must have something to show for all this.'

Little Lucy could not understand why Doctor Evans wanted to examine her. 'I'm, not ill,' she kept saying. 'There's nothing wrong with me.'

'Are you still ticklish?' asked the doctor. Lucy put her head on one side.

'Only sometimes,' she replied, grinning.

'What's all this I hear about you falling in the pond this morning?'

Lucy stamped her foot impatiently. 'I didn't,' she said angrily.

'Oh well, maybe you didn't,' agreed Doctor Evans amicably. 'You know something Lucy? I think you're the healthiest person I've looked at today. I can't find a thing wrong – not a spot or a bump or a lump! But,' he added, narrowing his eyes so that Lucy looked at him anxiously, 'I bet you're still ticklish!' He gave Lucy a quick tickle and told her to go back outside and play. Then he turned to Mr and Mrs King.

'There's not a mark on her. She's a perfectly normal four year old. I can't find anything wrong at all.' Mr King started to say something but Doctor Evans interrupted. 'I know this is difficult for you but it seems to me that you both saw something extraordinary happen to Lucy. She says nothing happened. I think that something peculiar did happen, but it happened to both of *you*, not to Lucy. You had a sort of shared dream, a very real dream: so real that both of you are sure it actually happened.' Doctor Evans looked from one to the other. 'It's the only sensible explanation I can think of,' he added, as he packed his little case.

Mr King stood up slowly. 'Thank you for coming Doctor, I hope we haven't wasted your time.' Doctor Evans frowned and smiled at the same time.

'Not at all. It's been most interesting.' He shook hands and left. Mr King went back to his wife, shaking his head.

'It wasn't a dream,' insisted Mrs King. 'It really happened.'

For a few days after that, the Kings kept a special eye on Lucy but nothing happened to her. As the weeks passed both parents began to wonder if they really had dreamed the whole thing. Lucy became five, six, then seven and still nothing happened.

Now the Kings had almost forgotten about her flying, simply because they didn't want to remember it. But then something happened that started the whole thing all over again.

2

Something Extra-special

Lucy King was now almost eight. Many things had happened since she fell in the pond. She was taller and looked even wilder than before. Her long, fair curls rampaged down the sides of her smudgy face. Lucy always appeared to be dirty and Mrs King despaired of keeping her clean. She was forever mending and washing and taking a damp face-cloth to Lucy's hands and face. Then she'd rub hard while Lucy squirmed and struggled.

'I just don't know how you manage to get yourself so dirty,' sighed Mrs King, a few days before Lucy's eighth birthday.

'I'm not really dirty,' said Lucy, rubbing at the streaks of dirt on her suntanned arms. 'I could get a lot dirtier, only I do try to keep clean.'

'I don't believe it!' mocked her mum.

'I do. I can't help it if there's dirt on the things I touch.' Lucy sniffed. 'People should keep them clean.'

Mrs King scrubbed hard at Lucy's cheeks. 'I don't see how you can keep mud and puddles and bits of old iron and useless car tyres clean,' she said. 'Those are the things that you play with and they'll always be dirty. Why don't you play with your friends and do clean things? I never got dirty when I was a child. We had too many good games to play.'

'I've got good games,' protested Lucy, trying to get away from the face-cloth.

'I don't think rolling in the mud is a good game unless you happen to be a hippopotamus, Lucy. And I don't think making camps inside dustbins is a good game either. Now listen, it's time you did your piano practice.'

'Oh no!' wailed Lucy, and she pulled a hideous face. At that moment Nicholas poked his small, dark head round the kitchen door. He grinned up at his sister.

'Piano practice,' he reminded her. 'Don't forget your piano practice.'

'You wait, Nicholas,' shouted Lucy, still struggling beneath the face-cloth.

Lucy had been taking piano lessons for two months. At first she thought it would be great because she would be able to play brilliantly straight away. In actual fact it was a lot harder than that. She was still finding it difficult to read music, let alone play it with two hands. Mum and Dad made her practise for half an hour every day and she hated it.

'I'm going to play in the garden,' announced Nicholas loudly, just to make Lucy jealous.

'Don't tease your sister,' said Mrs King. 'It's really not fair, Nicholas.'

Lucy stuck out her tongue and pulled another revolting face. Nicholas stared at her thoughtfully.

'You know that competition on TV about drawing a wild animal and you can win a bicycle?' he began.

'Yes? What about it?' muttered Lucy, with her face still twisted up horribly.

'Well, if you pull that face again I'm going to

draw you. Then I'll send it in. It's bound to win. I think I'll call it Wild Girl of the Woods. When they see it, they'll probably send an animal-catcher round to get you and take you to the zoo or something.'

'Ha ha, very funny,' sneered Lucy. 'Why don't you go and fall under a lorry?'

'Lucy!' cried Mum, quite horrified. 'Don't ever say things like that! That is a terrible thing to say to anybody, especially your own brother.'

Lucy was taken aback. She hadn't thought it was *that* awful. She and Nick were always saying things like that to each other. In fact they had a game they sometimes played where they tried to think of the most awful things that could happen to each other. Lucy reddened.

'Nick knows I didn't mean it,' she mumbled. Mrs King sighed.

'Don't call him Nick. His name is Nicholas.'

'But that takes ages to say,' complained Lucy. 'I mean, if there was a fire or something and you had to tell Nick, I mean Nicholas, something quickly, by the time you'd called out his name he would have got all frazzled up!' Lucy grinned at the thought.

'Don't be stupid,' snapped Mrs King. 'I don't know, first you want him run over by a lorry and now he's being burned to death. For goodness sake go and get on with your piano

practice before you think of some other awful ending for poor Nicholas.'

Lucy gave a long groan and stomped off to the front room. She shut the door, sat herself on the piano stool and fiddled with her music. First she looked at one piece and then another, but she didn't play anything. After five minutes of silence from the piano Mrs King shouted through the door. 'Get on with it!'

Lucy thumped out a simple tune with one finger. She had a brilliant idea. If she played her tunes twice as fast, then she should finish twice as quickly. It seemed to make sense, so Lucy raced through six different pieces. When she looked at the clock she was astonished to see how little time had passed. She sighed and stared out of the open window.

Nicholas was outside playing with their cat,

Flop. Lucy sat on her stool, her hands idle, watching the cat stalking a twig that Nicholas was trailing behind him. Then he found a conker from the previous year and began to toss it on the grass. Flop chased after it and batted it with her front paws. Lucy forgot all about her piano practice.

Nicholas picked up the conker and threw it even further. It bounced down the garden path and Flop shot after it. She flicked a paw at the little ball and sent it scuddering under the garden gate and into the road, where it spun round before lurching to a halt. Nicholas opened the gate and ran out to collect the conker, laughing at Flop who was still searching under the gate.

Lucy's little brother did not see or even hear the lorry coming down the road. He was too

busy thinking about his game with Flop. There was a shriek of screaming tyres as the lorry driver rammed his foot hard on the brakes, but there was nothing he could do. The uncontrollable vehicle skidded sideways – but it still went straight for the terror-struck Nicholas. An old lady walking on the pavement screeched and covered her face with both hands.

Suddenly Lucy appeared, her flying body shining with a bright red, crackling glow. She hurtled out of the window, toppling the piano stool. With both arms stretched out in front, and her long curls streaming behind, she zoomed down and swept Nicholas from beneath the whirling black tyres of the thundering lorry and carried him back safely to the garden. There she sat on the wall, grinning, while the red glow slowly faded and Nicholas stared up at her, still in a state of open-mouthed shock.

The little old lady took her hands from her face and fainted. The lorry came to a squealing halt and the driver jumped down and ran back to Lucy. He looked at her as if he had seen a ghost. His mouth worked up and down like a large fish's, but for a few moments he could say nothing. At last a stammering cry fell from his pale lips.

'Yu . . . yu . . . you all right?' The driver put a finger on Nicholas and then he touched Lucy to see if she was real. Lucy laughed.

'Yes,' she said. 'Of course we're all right.' She brushed one hand through her curls and there was a faint crackle of static electricity.

Mrs King came hurrying out of the house. Before she had time to ask what all the noise had been about, the lorry driver had told her. Together they picked up the old lady and brought her into the house for a strong cup of tea. The lorry driver had one too, because his legs felt a bit wobbly. Even Mrs King was a bit flustered.

'Like a bolt of lightning, she were,' murmured the old lady. 'Glowing she were, an' all. Glowing red all over, and sizzling and crackling like I don't know what.'

Mrs King looked out of the window to where Lucy was already playing quite normally with Nicholas. She hurriedly got rid of the old lady and the lorry driver. They kept asking awkward questions and Mrs King did not have any answers. When they had gone she called her children indoors.

'Lucy, tell me what happened out on the road.' Lucy burst into floods of tears.

'I didn't mean it Mum, really I didn't. I didn't know it would happen!'

'What on earth are you talking about?' asked Mum soothingly.

'She means the lorry,' explained Nicholas.

'But what about the lorry?'

'I didn't know there really would be a lorry trying to run Nicky over,' wailed Lucy. 'I know I said he ought to fall in front of a lorry but I didn't mean it to happen.'

Mrs King smiled and gave Lucy a big hug. 'Don't be silly,' she said softly. 'That lorry didn't come because of what you said to Nicholas. That was just chance. But what actually happened?' Nicholas began to jump up and down impatiently because Lucy was still sniffing.

'I ran into the road, only I didn't see this monster lorry coming. It was going to squash me but Lucy flew out of the front room and picked me up.'

'I'm sure you don't mean that Lucy *flew*, do you, Nicholas?'

'Of course I do!' he cried. 'She flew and she was all flashing red. It was very exciting Mum, I wish she'd do it again.'

Mrs King had become silent so Lucy went off quietly because she didn't want anything to remind Mum that she hadn't finished her piano practice. Dad got the whole story from Nicholas and Mrs King as soon as he got in from work. He asked Lucy about it too, and this time she remembered everything. Lucy wondered why everybody was making such a fuss about it all. It seemed quite natural to her. If somebody was about to get crushed by a lorry you rushed out and saved them.

'But Lucy, dear,' said Mrs King, 'children don't fly and glow red.' Lucy shrugged her shoulders.

'I can't help that. I mean, there's a boy at school called Richard and he can make both his ears waggle. He makes them go up and down and they wriggle and nobody else in the whole school can do that. I mean, you could say that children can't waggle their ears, but Richard can. He does it every playtime.' Lucy looked up at her parents and smiled. 'Anyway,' she added, 'it didn't make me dirty.' Mr King laughed but Mrs King shook her head.

'I think I would prefer it if you did just get dirty. At least I can understand that.' She sighed heavily. 'Oh well, let's have tea.'

That evening when both children were in bed, Mr and Mrs King talked for a long time.

'There's no explanation for it, but it's happened again,' said Mr King. 'It's not a dream. Our Lucy has something special, something extra-special.' Mrs King nodded slowly.

'I suppose we shall have to put up with it,' she said. 'But I do wish she could just be ordinary for one minute.'

3

Nicholas Takes Off

Mr King folded his newspaper, took off his reading glasses and looked across at Mrs King. 'I've just thought,' he said, 'do you remember when Lucy was six months old?' Without looking up from her work, Mrs King nodded. 'We were on holiday,' continued Mr King. 'We went out one afternoon for a wander round that little fishing village. Do you remember how it got terribly dark because of that sudden storm?'

'The thunder!' said Mrs King. 'And the lightning too. It was right above us, wasn't it, and it all started when we were in that little shop that sold those shell-thingummies. What were they?'

'Flower-pot holders.' Mr King leant forward and tapped his wife on one knee. 'Now tell me,' he said with a secretive smile, 'where was Lucy?'

'Where was Lucy?' repeated Mrs King. 'In her pram of course.'

'But where was the pram?' demanded her husband.

'It was outside. I remember it well because

when the thunder and lightning started we rushed out to her and just as we got to the door . . .' Mrs King trailed off into silence and for a few moments she stared at her husband. Then she whispered, 'Do you think that was it?'

'It could be,' said Mr King. 'There's got to be an explanation somewhere for Lucy's strange power.' His wife leaned forward eagerly.

'There was that awful clap of thunder right overhead wasn't there Harold? I thought it was the end of the world. Then an enormous flash of lightning and the whole of Lucy's pram seemed to glow and there was that dreadful sizzling noise. We rushed out to the pram and when we looked in, she was lying there and laughing. Do you remember?'

'I do, I do,' said Mr King. 'And then it simply poured. We were soaked and had to rush for the car. We even came home a day early.'

The couple looked at each other. 'It must have been that,' said Mrs King at last. 'There has to be a reason. Do you think Lucy's getting worse? All sorts of odd things have happened since she rescued Nicholas. She doesn't seem different herself, but things have happened.'

'What sort of things?'

'Nothing much, just little things. I keep going into rooms and getting a strange prickly sensation in the back of my neck, especially in Lucy's bedroom. It feels as if somebody is tweaking my hair from behind, but there's never anybody there. Yesterday I came out into the hall from the kitchen and I'm sure I saw a flash of red hurtle up the stairs, just like a ball of fire.'

'Ball of fire?' exclaimed Mr King. 'Perhaps it was Flop chasing something.'

Mrs King eyed her husband patiently. 'Flop is hardly like a ball of fire, dear. She's an old,

fluffy black and white cat. That's not what I saw at all.' Mr King grunted. It was too puzzling.

'Hmmm. Well I don't suppose it had anything to do with Lucy. It's her work at school that worries me. Her teacher says she's a lazy chatterbox who hardly ever reads and does the most awful, scruffy work.' He broke off and groaned.

'Well I don't find that at all surprising,' said Mrs King. 'She's exactly the same at home – untidy and lazy.' They both began to laugh and Mr King said, 'It's obvious that she hasn't changed at all!'

Lucy King had changed though. Ever since she had rescued Nicholas she had felt different somehow. At first she didn't think that there was anything special about flying and having crackling hair, but so many people seemed to think it was odd that Lucy found herself wondering about it more and more.

Early one morning she found herself alone at the adventure playground. She stood beside the swings and dreamily wondered if she could zoom over to the climbing frame, which was some distance away. Hardly had she thought it than she was there, standing next to the climbing frame as though nothing had happened. She wasn't even out of breath. Lucy watched

the flickering red flush fade away. To test herself further, she ran as fast as she could back to the swings. She arrived, several seconds later, panting as furiously as a tortoise at the Olympic Games. When at last she got her breath back, she flew in an instant back to the climbing frame and once more watched her fiery radiance slowly disappear. For the first time Lucy realised what she could do, and she was delighted.

Over the next week or so, Lucy did her zooming act in private whenever she could, though once Mum nearly caught her flying up the stairs. What Lucy did not know was that her wonderful powers made her capable of doing other things beside flying. She soon found out though.

One day she was upstairs in her bedroom, struggling to make a camp out of bedclothes by stretching them over an open cupboard door. Nicholas kept wandering in and out. He was being a bit of a nuisance.

'I can make a better camp than that!' he kept saying.

'Good. Go and make one in your own room then,' snapped Lucy.

'Can't I come in yours?'

'No.'

'I'll let you use my bow,' said Nicholas.

'I don't want your bow, I'm not Robin Hood. I'm me, and this is my camp and I want to be alone.'

'You won't be able to catch any food without my bow and arrow,' insisted Nicholas slyly.

'Look,' cried Lucy angrily, 'if I get your bow I'll shoot you and eat you. Go and play with a crocodile or something.'

'I want to come in your camp,' whined Nicholas, and he came nearer.

Almost without thinking, Lucy raised her arms and pointed her grubby, nail-bitten fingers at her brother. She did it in desperation, trying to keep him out of her private camp. Her hair stuck out at all angles and her body gently throbbed with a vivid red glow. Her eyes shone like black stars and tiny flickers of lightning sparked from her fingertips.

Nicholas found himself lifted from the ground and floating round Lucy's bedroom. She wasn't touching him, just pointing at him and grinning. Nicholas hovered over the chest of drawers. He kicked his legs and wailed.

'Put me down! Mum! Mum! Tell Lucy to put me down, it's not fair!'

There was a pounding of feet on the stairs as Mrs King hurried up. She ran into Lucy's bedroom and threw up her hands at the sight of Nicholas hovering round the room. She gawped at her son and then stared at Lucy who sat, quietly glowing, just inside her camp.

'Lucy!' cried her mum. 'Is this your doing? I might have known. Let Nicholas get down please.'

Lucy gave her mum a bright smile and then concentrated her strangely glowing eyes upon Nicholas. She made him do a double slow-motion somersault in mid-air and then landed him safely on the wardrobe.

'Not up there!' shouted Mrs King. 'On the floor, at once!' Lucy brought Nicholas down to ground level, where he immediately began to wail. The red glow vanished and Lucy shook out her curls with a tiny shower of sparks.

'I only wanted to go in her camp,' sobbed Nicholas, clutching at his mum.

'It's really too naughty, Lucy,' said Mrs King sternly. 'You mustn't play cruel tricks like that just because you have special powers. It's very unkind. You can stay up here until I call you for tea.' Mrs King pulled Nicholas out and shut the door with a bang.

Lucy retreated deep into her cupboard-camp and looked closely at her hands. She was delighted. Anyway, why should Nicholas and Mum be so cross about it? She couldn't help it. She hadn't meant to make Nicholas float like that. It had just happened.

Lucy idly pointed one finger at her teddy. He took off slowly and then zoomed upwards. He cruised round the room and finally dived out of one corner and landed in Lucy's lap.

She hugged it closely. A voice shouted up the stairs. 'Lucy! Tea-time!'

She went down and sat at the big kitchen table.

'Say you're sorry to Nicholas,' said Mrs King.

'Sorry Nicky,' said Lucy, helping herself to some bread.

'Not Nicky! How many times do I have to tell you? His name is Nicholas.'

'Muhmuhmuss,' mumbled Lucy through a mouthful of bread and jam.

Mrs King once more turned on her daughter. 'Your manners are dreadful,' she scolded. Lucy eyed her, wishing that she dared to make her mother float across the table and round the room like her teddy had just done upstairs. Mrs King almost laughed.

'I know what you're thinking, Lucy King, so don't you dare. If you can do special things you make sure you keep them for the right time.'

Lucy frowned. 'I can't even think in this house without someone knowing all about it.'

'Never mind. Have some more bread,' suggested Mum. 'You're being very quiet Nicholas.'

'I've got tummy-ache,' he said, looking at Lucy with a meaningful stare.

'I'll give you some medicine,' said Mum, reaching up into the cupboard. The small brown bottle was wedged behind the best teapot. As Mrs King pulled it out, the pot got pushed to the edge of the shelf and toppled over.

'No!' cried Mrs King in horror.

Lucy calmly raised one sparking finger towards the falling pot and the fat teapot stopped, a few centimetres above the stone tiles. Lucy made the pot turn up the right way and then she flew it three times round the room before allowing it to land gracefully on the kitchen table.

Mrs King let out the long breath she had been holding all this time.

'Thank you Lucy,' she said at last.

'It was a special occasion,' said Lucy.

'Yes, it certainly was. I don't think you had to make it fly round the room so many times though. That was showing off.' Lucy blushed and looked down at her jam sandwich. Nicholas began pointing at the teapot, jabbing at it with each of his fingers in turn.

'Why can't I do it?' he demanded.

'I think one person in the family is quite enough for that sort of activity,' murmured Mrs King. 'Absolutely enough.'

4

The Christmas Angel

Lucy enjoyed school except for two things. One was work and the other was Maureen Best. Lucy didn't know why Mr Barber, her teacher, made her sit next to Maureen. Maureen was one of those girls who seemed to be brilliant at everything and it made her rather big-headed. The two girls didn't like each other at all. Maureen thought Lucy was the biggest clot on earth and Lucy said Maureen looked like a mouldy apricot.

The whole school was preparing for Christmas. Decorations were being put up everywhere and each class was making something. Lucy got quite involved.

'Look,' said Maureen one dark afternoon. 'I've made six of those bell-things.'

Lucy looked at the bells jealously. She had only managed to make one. She had tried desperately hard and yet it had still turned out looking as if a herd of elephants had played football with it.

'Is that all you've done!' smirked Maureen. 'It's all squashed. I don't suppose Mr Barber will hang that up.' Neither did Lucy suppose so. None of her work ever got put on display.

Maureen held two of her beautiful bells up to the light and swung them from side to side. 'Really Lucy, you can't do anything. I suppose you want me to give you one of my spare bells? Well, if you give me all your crisps at playtime tomorrow you can have this one.' Maureen

held up a rather crumpled bell. Even crumpled, it looked a lot better than Lucy's, but was it worth a whole packet of crisps?

Lucy saw Mr Barber coming round, choosing the bells to decorate the classroom. She glanced back at Maureen's bell.

'All right,' she said, and hurriedly put the bell in front of her. Maureen grinned and sniffed at the same time.

'Don't forget tomorrow, the whole packet!' Lucy nodded and gritted her teeth. It was blackmail. Why did she have to sit next to the mouldy apricot?

Mr Barber came and stood behind Lucy. He bent down and looked at her bell.

'Well done,' he said, sounding surprised. 'You must have tried very hard, Lucy. It's lovely to see you making such an effort.' Each one of his words grated on Lucy's nerves and she wished she had never made the exchange at all. Maureen sniggered to herself while Mr Barber took the bell away and hung it up.

Lucy shut her eyes and wished that she could make Maureen Best float up into the sky and disappear for ever. She hoped Maureen would choke on the crisps.

Mr Barber began talking to the class about a Christmas play he wanted them to perform. He needed several actors. The announcement got everyone excited.

'Sssh,' said Mr Barber calmly. 'It's not easy to act. Some of you will have speeches to learn.' Lucy waved both hands wildly in the air. She just loved acting and having lots of people watching what she was doing, and she knew she could be brilliant at it.

Mr Barber wrote down the names of all the children who wanted to act and then he set about testing them. He gave them a piece of writing to read out loudly from the back of the class. 'Pretend you are on stage,' he suggested. 'I want to hear a nice loud, clear voice.'

One by one, the children read. Some did it well and some were even better. Maureen was one of the best of course. Some children were quieter than rioting snails. Then it was Lucy's turn. She spoke up really loudly because she was desperate to get herself a speaking part. Mr Barber clapped his hands over both ears.

'There's no need to shout that loudly,' he interrupted. 'They'll hear you in China!' The class thought this was hilarious and Lucy turned deep red. After that she could hardly

speak at all. It came out in a nervous whisper. Lucy knew she wouldn't be chosen and felt totally miserable.

Mr Barber didn't tell the children which ones had been chosen until the next day. Maureen got the part of the Angel Gabriel and the rest of the speaking parts went to other children. Lucy's was the last name to be called. She'd been given the part of a dumb angel. Lucy groaned. That meant she'd have cardboard wings and a halo made from a tin-foil pie-dish. She'd have to look saintly the whole evening. That wasn't acting at all. Maureen brushed past.

'I'm the Angel Gabriel,' she beamed. 'Have you got those crisps?' Lucy handed over the packet without a word. Maureen examined it carefully.

'They're all broken!' she complained. Lucy looked up at her.

'Oh,' she sighed, 'but you're so clever Maureen. Surely you can stick them back together again?' Maureen's eyes narrowed, but she could not think of an answer and turned on her heels and clicked away.

Every day now there were rehearsals. Mr Barber got crosser and crosser as children could not remember their lines or did the wrong thing. Mothers at home busily made costumes.

Mrs King made a superb angel dress for Lucy and her dad made a splendid pair of golden wings out of gold foil paper and thick card. It was a lot better than Lucy had imagined and she got quite excited by the idea of her costume and the performance. Then there came a bitter blow.

Mr Barber announced that the Angel Gabriel was going to use the brand new flying wire that the school had recently bought for the stage. There was a gasp of envy from the rest of the class and Maureen grinned like a drunken pig. The flying wire was a belt with a wire attached that went to a strong beam in the ceiling. If you buckled the belt around your waist you could be hoisted safely up into the air over the stage, so that it seemed you were really flying.

Of course, everyone had wanted to try it, but Maureen was going to be the lucky one.

'Why does everything happen to her?' whispered one of the naughtiest boys.

'Because she's such an angel of course,' answered Lucy quickly, and she flapped her hands like a pair of wings. The boy laughed, but they were both still envious, even when Maureen found it difficult to speak because the belt cut into her lungs. Her face went rather red.

'She's not the Angel Gabriel,' Lucy told her mum. 'She's the Beetroot Gabriel.'

The day of the performance came at last. The excited children watched the school hall fill with parents – a real, live audience. They dashed back to their classes to get their costumes on. Mr Barber checked the flying wire to make certain it was safe. The audience went quiet as the hall lights were dimmed. The curtains were pulled aside and the play began.

Everything went well to start with. Only once did a shepherd forget a line. There was a short pause and then one of the other actors covered up for him. Mr Barber breathed a sigh of relief. It was almost time for the angels to go on. He tightened the belt round Maureen's waist.

'Good luck!' he whispered and started up the machinery to hoist Maureen over the stage.

Then it all went wrong. The machinery jammed solid and would not budge. The actors on stage waited in tense silence for the Angel Gabriel to lead the other angels on. It was supposed to be the highlight of the show, with the Angel Gabriel flying high above the cast. The audience waited, knowing that something had gone wrong. Mr Barber threw up his hands in despair.

'It's no good,' he said. 'You'll have to go on just as you are.' At this point the Angel Gabriel burst into loud sobs because she felt so let down.

'Pull yourself together!' hissed Mr Barber anxiously, while the whole cast waited. 'These things happen. Just go on as you are.' But Maureen cried even louder.

Lucy had a horrible thought. If she wished, she could make Maureen float up to the ceiling after all. Then everybody would see the wailing Angel Gabriel with tears smudging her very un-angelic face. No, that would be nasty. Lucy tugged at Mr Barber's sleeve as he sent the other angels on stage to keep things going.

'I know all Maureen's lines,' she murmured. Mr Barber gazed at her for a second. He made his decision and smiled.

'Good girl Lucy, are you sure?' Lucy nodded. Mr Barber patted her halo.

'Right, on you go then!' Lucy grinned up at her teacher. It was an enormous grin, from one ear to the other.

'Not on,' she said. 'Up!' Mr Barber's eyes bulged like stupefied marbles as Lucy rose gracefully into the air and flew slowly across the stage with her hair sparkling just like a real halo.

Then she began her speech, hovering over everyone's head. She did it marvellously. When she finished, the audience actually cheered. They thought the flying was very effective and didn't realise the machine had broken down.

Mr Barber was the only one who knew the truth. Lucy flew across the stage several times while the audience clapped continuously. At last she flew off, closely followed by the cast.

As soon as she got backstage Lucy asked 'Where's Mr Barber?' She wanted to find out if her performance had been all right.

'Oh!' cried one of the other angels. 'He fainted when you took off. He's been taken to the staffroom to lie down.'

Mr and Mrs King, who had been in the audience, had also hurried to the staffroom to see Mr Barber. When they had seen Lucy fly across the stage they knew instantly that there was no machine holding their extraordinary daughter up, especially when she did it three times.

'She's a show-off,' whispered Mrs King to her husband.

'So would you be if you could fly,' replied Mr King with a proud smile.

In the staffroom they had an urgent, hushed conference.

'We want it kept a secret,' explained Mrs King. 'We don't want Lucy to get big ideas about herself.'

'We'd rather as few people know about her powers as possible,' said Mr King.

'Of course,' said the white faced teacher. 'I'm not sure I believe what I saw myself.'

Back in the hall the play ended triumphantly. The audience clapped and clapped. Maureen had already been taken home with an awful headache and had missed the fun. Back in the classrooms the children changed out of their costumes and talked excitedly about the performance.

'What was the flying machine like, Lucy?' asked one of her friends.

Lucy was just going to tell them all what had really happened when she saw her parents coming through the door. She frowned for a moment.

'Well the belt was a bit tight,' she said quickly. 'But I managed.'

'You were brilliant,' one of them said. Lucy blushed deep red.

Mr King laughed and shook his head. 'I don't know, Lucy. Whoever would have thought you'd be a success as an angel of all things!'

5

The Outing

Lucy came home from school very excited one day. She burst through the front door and ran to the kitchen, where Mum was peeling potatoes.

'Mum! Mum! We're going on an outing and we need sandwiches and a drink – only we can't take tins and it costs 65p and Paula says I can sit next to her so we can share sweets – only I mustn't take barley-sugars because Paula doesn't like barley-sugars and . . .' She drew in a deep breath.

Mrs King put down the potato peeler and waited for quiet. 'I don't know how you manage to think about what you're saying Lucy. It comes out like a volcanic eruption. Calm down and tell me again. Where are you going?'

'To the Priory Museum.'

Mum nodded. 'And when are you going?'

'Next Monday, and I've got to wear my best clothes,' said Lucy.

'I should think so too. What are you going to do at the museum?' Lucy looked blankly at her mother. 'Don't you know? Surely Mr Barber told you?'

Lucy thought for a moment. 'I think so,' she said at last. 'I think he said something about stinking eggs and hairy manners but it didn't make sense and that's why I didn't listen.' Mum began to scratch at the potatoes again.

'Really Lucy, you are useless. You don't listen to a word. It goes in one ear . . .'

'And out the other,' interrupted Lucy. 'I know Mum. You keep telling me.'

'I'd better give Paula's mum a ring. Perhaps Paula listens to Mr Barber when he tells you things.'

'That's because she's a goody-goody and always gets everything right,' said Lucy quickly.

Mrs King went to the telephone and spoke to Paula's mum for several minutes. Lucy heard her laughing. When Mrs King came back to the kitchen she was still smiling. She gave Lucy a playful clump on the head.

'You really are the end, Lucy. Honestly, what did you think you were going to see at the museum – "stinking eggs and hairy manners?" Mr Barber said that you are going to see extinct hairy mammoths and a lot of other fossils too.'

'Oh!' said Lucy, idly making Mum's potatoes fly slowly over the table and land with little plops in the pan of boiling water on the stove. Mrs King gave a long sigh.

'I do wish you wouldn't do that. I find it so

muddling Lucy. I'm just not used to flying potatoes yet.'

'Sorry.' Lucy dragged herself out of the kitchen.

It seemed ages before Monday came. Lucy had packed everything she needed at least two days too early. Mum refused to make the sandwiches until the night before. Lucy insisted on helping, so it took twice as long.

On the Monday morning the class crowded onto a big coach and spent five minutes sorting out which seats they wanted. All the boys wanted to go in the long seat at the back, but Lucy didn't mind where she was. Mr Barber and two parents came in the coach too. It was exciting, and Lucy kept bouncing up and down in her seat until Mr Barber told her to sit still before she bounced out of the window.

Lucy thought it was better being in a coach than in a car because she could see over all the hedges and walls.

'That's the bakery,' Paula pointed out. 'My uncle works there.'

'What does he do?'

'He puts the jam in doughnuts.' Lucy looked very surprised.

'He doesn't do it very well,' she said. 'He must get jam all over his trousers and the floor too because he keeps missing.' Paula was puzzled.

'What are you talking about?' she demanded.

'Well,' said Lucy with a big grin, 'when my mum buys doughnuts there's just a hole in the middle. There's no jam in them at all!'

'You're mad!' cried Paula. 'Those are ring-

doughnuts, not jam-doughnuts. Ring-doughnuts have holes and jam-doughnuts have jam . . .' By the time Paula had finished explaining they had reached the museum, and the tour began.

There were all sorts of odd things to see. There were fossil elephant teeth and bones and old flints that had been used as axes and spears. There were lots of drawings, too, that showed how people had lived thousands of years ago. Lucy peered closely at a painting of a hunting expedition.

'I bet Nicholas would have liked to be a stone-age hunter,' she said. 'He could have used his bow and arrow then.'

'They didn't have bows and arrows,' said Paula briskly, busily writing lots of notes in her pad. 'Look at that sabre-tooth tiger,' she added. Lucy gazed at the model of the extinct creature, with its enormous front fangs poking down the sides of its lower jaw. Mr Barber gathered the class around the animal.

'Why do you think it had teeth that long?' he asked them all.

'I bet he didn't like going to the dentist,' whispered Lucy to Paula, but her friend didn't even laugh.

'They didn't have dentists in those days,' she answered seriously.

'I know that!' cried Lucy. Really she wasn't *that* stupid.

'Did you say you know, Lucy?' asked Mr Barber in surprise. 'Can you tell us why the sabre tooth tiger had such long teeth?' Lucy blushed and stared wildly all over the museum. She suddenly remembered a TV programme about how parrots used their beaks for climbing through thick, leafy trees.

'Did they use them for climbing trees, Mr Barber?' she suggested brightly.

There was loud laughter. Even Mr Barber smiled.

'I don't think so,' he said. 'They were used for killing their prey.'

So the tour continued. Lucy began to think she would die of starvation if they didn't stop for lunch soon. At last they were allowed to go off to the little cafeteria and eat their sandwiches. 'I helped make these,' said Lucy with pride as she opened her sandwich box. Paula glanced inside.

'I can see that,' she agreed. 'They look bigger than bricks.'

After lunch there was little time for further exploration. Lucy was quite pleased because her legs ached. She was glad to get back on the coach. The journey back took about an hour, and it was up and down all the way. There was one exciting bit that Lucy enjoyed, even when she was in her dad's car. There was a particularly steep hill.

On the way to the museum you had to go up and round and up and round and the coach would get slower and slower until you thought it would start going backwards, but eventually it always got to the top. On the way back to school it was like diving off a mountainside because the coach would go streaming down the hill at breakneck speed and the driver would keep stamping on the brakes to slow the heavy vehicle down.

That's what the coach driver was doing today. He kept pushing at the brake pedal. He kept pushing and pushing and his face turned green and then white. Mr Barber leant forward, gripping the shuddering hand rail in front of him.

'What's the matter?' he asked.

'Brakes gone!' croaked the driver, plunging his foot up and down on the useless pedal. 'We haven't got any brakes!'

'Can't you do something?'

'I'm trying! I'm trying!' shouted the driver. Sweat poured from his face. 'Nothing!' he cried. 'We're getting faster and faster. We can't take the next bend at this speed. We're going to crash!'

Mr Barber leapt into the swinging aisle of the coach.

'Listen,' he yelled above the rising whine of the tortured tyres. 'Do what I say immediately. Lie down on the floor and wrap your arms round your heads. The coach is out of control. Get down on the floor immediately.'

The children started screaming at each other, but they did as Mr Barber had told them, all except for Lucy. She stared out of the front window in horror, watching the sharp bend racing relentlessly towards them. Paula reached up and tugged at her.

'Get down Lucy!' shouted Paula.

'Oh shut-up!' said Lucy, losing all patience. She desperately tried to concentrate on the coach, trying to make it stop. Somehow she could not make it work. Nothing she did had any effect upon the hurtling tons of metal. She struggled from her seat, clutching at the seats around her, for the coach was lurching violently from one side of the road to the other.

'Get down!' yelled Mr Barber from beneath his seat, but Lucy ignored him. She hauled herself to the front, right next to the driver.

'Let me out,' she asked. The driver didn't dare look up as he tried to keep his grip on the shaking steering wheel. 'Let me out!' shouted Lucy. The driver gave a wild laugh. He thought

Lucy was trying to escape.

'Won't do you any good jumping, Miss,' he shouted back. The corner was getting closer and closer. 'This is it!' the driver yelled.

Lucy's frantic eyes suddenly noticed the button marked DOOR amongst the driver's controls. She lunged forward and banged it with her fist. The door hissed open and the wind came screaming in. Before the driver could open his mouth, Lucy had zoomed out of the coach.

She rocketed forward, hovering a few metres in front of the coach. Her hair stuck out

straight, with masses of sparks scattering through the air, and she glowed as she had never done before. Power surged through her small body and passed out through her spread hands. She concentrated her whole being upon slowing down the helpless vehicle. The whole coach seemed to become enveloped by the flickering radiance that surrounded her body.

Gradually the coach slowed. The driver's eyes were riveted upon the vision of the glowing girl floating in front of him. He felt the control of the vehicle coming back. Mr Barber and the children struggled from the floor and sat in their seats. They could not take their eyes off Lucy hovering in front, still guiding the coach. Even the crying had stopped. At last the coach halted.

Lucy flew back to the roadside and the red flush faded. She shook her crackling hair back into shape with a shower of dying sparks and climbed up the steps into the coach.

'Lucy King . . .' began Mr Barber. He coughed. Words had caught in his throat. He didn't know what to say. Lucy smiled sheepishly at everybody.

'Where are my brick sandwiches?' she asked. 'I'm hungry.'

6

Pruno!

Of course, after the adventure with the coach, the secret of Lucy's strange and wonderful powers could not be kept hidden any longer. Within twenty-four hours Mr and Mrs King found themselves answering never-ending knocks at the door and telephone calls. Everybody in the King household got a headache, including Lucy. Mrs King began to wish that her daughter had never been left out in that thunderstorm eight years earlier.

The story of the uncontrollable coach and Lucy's glowing display of flying filled the newspapers for several days. The King family could not move from the house without being questioned by reporters, or photographed. They stayed indoors as much as possible and began to feel like prisoners in their own house.

Lucy wondered how she could have caused so much fuss and the more dismayed her parents became, the more Lucy felt she was to blame. Then, suddenly, one morning all the press men and TV crews had gone. There wasn't a reporter in sight. It turned out that a polar bear at

London Zoo had just given birth to a black bear-cub and they had all gone to write about that.

However, when the post arrived their peace was broken once more. Letters simply poured through the letter-box. Lucy started to get all sorts of requests. A building firm asked if she could use her super-strength to knock down some old houses that needed demolishing. It would save them a lot of time and money. Another letter came from a part of the country that had received no rain for two months. Would Lucy please push some clouds over their bit of the country and hold them there until they had emptied?

There were many more letters asking for help and also several from companies that wanted Lucy to appear on television and advertise their products. Mr King tore them all up without bothering to read them. It didn't stop the endless flood of mail though. The postman didn't bother to push them through the letter-box any longer. He just left a sack full of letters on the Kings' doorstep.

One evening they sat at the tea-table in gloomy silence. Mrs King sighed.

'I wish we could get away somewhere, just for a little while.' She glanced apprehensively at her husband.

'We can't,' he said. 'We simply haven't got the money.'

'I've got 72p in my money box,' offered Nicholas.

'And I've got 40p,' said Lucy. Mr King gave them a tired smile.

'I'm afraid it's not enough. No, we just don't have the money to go away, especially after that last bill I had to pay on the car.'

Silence spread round the table once more. Mrs King stared out of the window.

'Lucy could get us some money,' Nicholas suggested.

'How?' asked Lucy.

'You could break into a bank with your super-strength and take the money.'

'Ha ha. Anyway, I'm not super-strong. I can only sort of levitate things.'

'Well levitate the money out of the bank then,' said Nicholas.

'I wish I could levitate a brain into your head,' said Lucy sharply. 'I don't know if you know this Nicholas, but it's against the law to rob banks.'

'Well why don't you do one of those adverts on TV then?' persisted Nicholas.

'What adverts?'

'The ones that Dad keeps tearing up. You can get money for that.'

Mrs King sat up straight and stared at her son. 'How do you know all this, Nicholas?' she asked.

'I've read all the bits in the litter bin.'

'Ugh!' cried Lucy, but she was interrupted by Mum.

'Tell us what they said,' demanded Mrs King, eagerly leaning forward. Nicholas thought carefully for a second.

'Um . . . the only one I can remember was about some wallpaper and they said they'd pay Lucy £500 for making a TV advert.' Mrs King's eyes widened. She stared at her husband but he shook his head.

'Lucy's not going to make adverts,' he said. 'They'll spoil her and make her feel special. They'll make fools of all of us.'

'But £500!' whispered Mrs King.

'I don't mind making an advert!' Lucy cried, jumping up and down.

'We could go away for two weeks!' murmured Mrs King dreamily. 'We could go abroad. Right away to another country . . .'

'In an aeroplane!' shouted Nicholas. 'We could fly!' Lucy groaned.

'I can do that already,' she complained in such a fed-up voice that everybody laughed. Mr King looked from one happy face to the next.

'All right, I give in. Let's have a look at those torn up letters.'

Mum got some tape and they began to stick the letter-litter back together. An hour later they found what they were looking for. They had read several rather silly offers but this one seemed fairly sensible. A big cereal firm were about to launch a new breakfast cereal called PRUNO. The firm offered Lucy £800 to make a TV advert for them.

'£800!' cried Nicholas, dancing round the room.

'£800!' cried Mrs King as she joined him. Then Lucy began a dance too, while Mr King watched them with a worried smile. He wasn't convinced they were doing the right thing. All the same, he wrote to Nutt & Co, the cereal firm, that same evening.

A week later Lucy found herself on a train, going to London with Mum. They were due at the TV studios to film the advert. They were met at the London station by Mr Nutt himself and he took them off in his silver Rolls-Royce. Mr Nutt was a very friendly fat man. Lucy couldn't help wondering if he was so portly because he had to test lots of cereals. Mr Nutt chatted to the Kings all the way there.

'PRUNO is going to be a big hit, Mrs King. It's a wonderful new cereal!'

'What's in it?' asked Lucy.

'Crunchy wheat-flakes, rolled oats and succulent slivers of dried prune,' answered Mr Nutt with a beaming red-faced smile.

Lucy was horrified. She couldn't stand prunes. She loathed them. Mrs King knew exactly what poor Lucy was thinking and she whispered in her ear.

'I don't suppose you'll have to eat any dear. Just think, £800! Our first holiday for six years. It will only take a couple of minutes, I'm sure.'

Mrs King sounded as if she were calming Lucy before a visit to the dentist, but Lucy felt much worse than that. She sat back in the purring car thinking of slivers of dried prune. Her stomach gave an ominous grumble.

At the studio there were many more people

than Lucy would have imagined necessary for making a film. There were cameramen, sound men, a director wearing an enormous tartan cloth-cap, and lots of other people wandering around. A make-up lady spurted powder all over Lucy's face and put lipstick on her too.

'Right,' shouted the director, waving his arms above his head. 'Are we ready, everybody?' He looked at Lucy. 'Haven't you got your costume on yet?'

'What costume?' Lucy asked.

'Oh come on! Time's money in this business little girl. You lot always have costumes. Look at Batman and Robin. You know what I mean.'

Lucy had taken an instant dislike to the director. She looked helplessly at her mum.

'She doesn't have a costume,' murmured Mrs King. 'She does it as she is.'

The director practically exploded on the spot. 'What! Doesn't she twirl round and there's a flash and she re-appears in a flying suit or something?' Mrs King and Lucy both shook their heads.

'Why didn't anybody tell me this before!' screeched the director. 'Don't you even sprout wings?'

'No,' said Lucy, almost in tears.

'Oh ruin!' cried the director, and he collapsed back in his chair. Luckily Mr Nutt came to the rescue.

'It really doesn't matter at all,' he said, beaming his big smile. 'All we want you to do is this. You come to the table and sit down for breakfast. You pour some PRUNO onto your plate and take a couple of mouthfuls. You look amazed at the wonderful taste and start rising up into the air as if it's PRUNO that has given you some special power. You go zooming through the ceiling.' Lucy looked up at the ceiling in alarm.

'Don't worry, it's made of strong paper. When you burst through the paper you'll find tons of PRUNO flakes up there and they'll come raining down onto the table, making a spectacular end to the advert. All right?' He beamed at Lucy. She nodded and looked at the groaning director. Mr Nutt bent down and whispered to her.

'Don't worry about him. He's always like that. Take no notice.' Lucy smiled gratefully, and the filming went ahead.

Lucy walked up to the table and poured out her breakfast. She took a large spoonful of PRUNO and put it in her mouth, smiling at the whirring camera. She chewed the cereal for a moment and then suddenly turned green. Her eyes bulged, her nose shrivelled up and with a dreadful splutter she spat the offending cereal out. 'Urrrgh!' she cried, wiping her mouth vigorously.

'Cut!' screamed the director, tearing wildly at his hair. 'What do you think you're doing, you idiot?'

'It's horrible,' cried Lucy. 'I couldn't help it.'

'Really Lucy,' said Mrs King lamely. Mr Nutt had hidden his face in his hands.

'You've ruined it!' shouted the director,

leaping from his chair so that it went toppling backwards. He was almost berserk with rage.

'I told you I couldn't help it,' sobbed Lucy with tears in her eyes. 'I never did like prunes, and please don't shout at me like that.'

'Raaargh!' choked the director in his fury. He plucked his cloth cap from his head and hurled it at Lucy. She instinctively dodged the tartan missile by zooming up into the air.

She burst through the paper ceiling and a moment later the TV studio was rapidly disappearing beneath an endless downpour of PRUNO flakes. The camera crew tried to escape, crunching their way through the fallen flakes. One of them tripped over an electric cable. As he tried to stop himself falling, he accidentally switched on the wind-machine. A howling gale instantly turned the downpour into a whirling

T.V
PRUN

blizzard as PRUNO flakes whizzed round the studio, burying everything in sight.

Lucy crouched up amongst the rafters of the roof and watched with dismay. At last Mr Nutt managed to switch the wind-machine off and the flakes slowly settled. The studio floor was a deep sea of PRUNO. Parts of the sea stirred and crackled and heaved as people got back to their feet. The director was found sobbing quietly beneath a mound of soggy flakes.

'It's not fair!' he kept saying. 'I can't find my cap.'

Lucy drifted down from the rafters and joined her mother. Mr Nutt sadly took them out to his car. There was silence on the journey. It was not until they reached the station that Mr Nutt spoke. He tried to beam a smile at Lucy.

'It's not your fault,' he said kindly. 'I know PRUNO is revolting. I can't stand it myself. Still, you do realise we can't pay you?' Lucy nodded.

'Goodbye Lucy,' said Mr Nutt, and he shook her hand, turned and disappeared into the crowd on the platform.

'Goodbye £800,' whispered Mrs King, but Lucy heard her. She sat back in her seat on the train and looked at her mother's tired face.

Tears welled up in her eyes and she couldn't stop them from rolling down her cheeks, not even with her special powers. It was all her fault. No money, no holiday. She had spoilt things for the whole family. The tears came faster and faster.

Mrs King sat next to her daughter and put an arm round her heaving shoulders. She was dabbing at her own eyes with a little handkerchief.

'Sssh,' sniffed Mrs King. 'It's not your fault Lucy. Forget all about it. I thought that director was the most ill-mannered, horrible person I've ever come across.' Mrs King gave a sudden laugh. 'He was even worse than Nicholas!' Lucy laughed a bit then, despite all her tears.

7

Thunder and Lightning Lucy

Lucy lay in bed with her head buried beneath her pillow.

'Do you think she's ill?' Mrs King asked her husband at the breakfast table. 'It's not like Lucy to lie in bed.'

'I know,' grunted Mr King. 'Usually she's up at 6 o'clock, waking everybody by leaping on them.' Mrs King tried to smile. Her husband continued. 'Leave her be. She's upset because of the advert failure.'

'I think we're all upset, Harold. What are we going to do? We put a £100 deposit on a holiday because we thought Lucy would get that advertisement money. Now we can't go on holiday after all. What will happen?'

Mr King stared glumly at the table-cloth. 'We shall just have to cancel the holiday,' he said in a flat voice.

'But what will happen to our £100 deposit?'

Mr King answered her bluntly. 'Oh we'll lose that. Gone. Nothing we can do about it.'

A long silence filled the room. Mr and Mrs King tried not to look at each other. They didn't want to see the dismay they both felt. At last Mr King spoke. He reached out one hand and laid it over his wife's hands.

'This is what we'll do. We shall go up to the High Street this morning and cancel the holiday. It's cattle-market day so the kids can watch that, while we do the worst bit. Then we'll go to that little café near the market and have a bite to eat. In the afternoon we'll all go to the cinema and forget our worries. The kids will like the pictures.'

Mrs King thought it was a splendid idea and when Lucy heard the news she jumped out of bed immediately. Nicholas was excited too.

'What's on at the cinema, Dad?' asked Lucy, already full of energy.

'I bet it's a real scarey film,' hinted Nicholas. 'I expect Lucy will hide under her seat. Did you know that she's afraid of cabbage?'

'I'm not!' yelled Lucy indignantly. 'You're an idiot.'

'You are. You're afraid of cabbage because the last time we had cabbage at school you put your hands over your face and started trembling.'

'All right, all right, break it up,' said Dad. 'I'll tell you what's on. It's a film called *Lightning Never Strikes Twice*. It's an adventure film about some jewel thieves or something.'

'Great!' said both kids, agreeing with each other for once.

The family decided to walk up to the High Street since it wasn't too far. Mum glanced out of the window before they left. 'Coats on, everybody,' she said. 'It looks like rain.'

The clouds were building up heavily. They glowered above, purple and angry, making the street quite dark.

'The weather is as gloomy as I feel,' murmured Mr King to his wife.

'I feel the same,' she said. 'Never mind, Lucy and Nicholas have cheered up.'

They left the two children at the market and went on ahead to the travel agent, where they waited sadly at the counter to be attended to. The travel agent said he was sorry they were cancelling their holiday.

'You do realise,' he continued, 'that you will

lose your £100 deposit?' Mr King just nodded. His wife put one arm through his, and pulled him away from the counter.

'Come on,' she said, trying to sound cheerful. 'Let's grab a cup of coffee.'

When they got outside it seemed darker than ever. Down at the market Lucy and Nicholas were having a good time. Lucy had quite forgotten about the disaster at the TV studio, and was running around madly, with Nicholas close at her heels.

'Look at those turkeys,' shouted Nicholas, pointing at a turkey-pen. 'They look as if they've just spilt rhubarb tart down their fronts.'

Then they climbed up some railings and peered over at three enormous white pigs, snuffling around in the straw.

'Help!' cried Lucy suddenly.

'What's up?' asked Nicholas in alarm.

'A pig's escaped!' Two nearby farmers stared all around. So did Nicholas.

'Where?' he cried. 'Where is it?'

'There!' shouted Lucy, pointing straight at her brother. He groaned.

'I suppose you think that's funny.' The two farmers were nudging each other and smiling. Nicholas tried to change the subject.

'Do you think it's going to rain? It's awfully dark.' Lucy glanced at the massing clouds. There was a rumble of thunder in the distance and a flash of lightning. The children looked for Mr and Mrs King. They weren't afraid of the approaching storm, but they didn't want to get wet.

Nicholas spotted them at the far side of the market and they ran over to join them, just as the first spots of rain began to fall. The cattle began to moo noisily. The thunder and lightning made them restless. They flicked their tails irritably and banged against the sides of their pens.

There was a sudden, blinding flash of lightning that slammed down on the market, followed immediately by a deafening explosion across the sky. The market animals exploded in their own chaotic way. Hens squawked and flapped, sending puffs of feathers up in the air. Sheep bleated and charged round their pens. The cattle bellowed and banged against their railings, which rocked furiously. Another hiss of lightning overhead made the cows charge at the railings again, and this time the sides of the pen fell away. Suddenly there were cows all over the market.

Kicking their frightened heels and mooing at the tops of their lungs, the lumbering beasts thundered out of the market and clattered up the High Street. Behind them came a long trail of puffing, shouting and waving farmers.

The storm got under way. The rain fell like bullets, bouncing from the hard road. Both cows and farmers were soaked. Lightning flickered continuously, as if a giant fuse in the sky had just blown. It became impossible to tell when one clatter of thunder finished and the next started.

The cows careered up the High Street, swerved round cars and scattered shoppers. Women screamed as they dragged their children to safety. Drivers hooted and skidded and crashed into lamp-posts, into each other and into shop-fronts, as they desperately tried to avoid being trampled by the galloping beasts. Some of the cattle appeared to get bored with the High Street. They lurched to one side and dashed into a supermarket.

Till-girls screamed and ran into the manager's office. The manager came running out, shouting and waving a newspaper. The cows took no notice. They were far too busy doing their shopping. They cannoned into displays of tins. They squashed great mounds of fruit beneath their clumping hooves. They skidded on the soggy mess they had just made and sat on the potted plants. Then they played bumper cars with the shopping trolleys, sending them crashing into each other. The cows bellowed and charged back into the High Street.

'Go away,' moaned the manager as he collapsed into a shopping trolley.

The High Street was in chaos. The cattle were thundering everywhere, trying to get into the smallest shops. Above the sound of the storm came the hubbub of shouts and breaking glass, mooing and snapping wood.

When Lucy saw the High Street, she could not stop herself from acting. Her hair crackled with a shower of sparks. The red glow shimmered round her body. She stood for a moment

letting her powers fill right up and then she took to the air and zoomed over amazed heads.

At the top of the High Street there was a statue of some famous townsman. Lucy swooped down and landed upon the statue's shoulders. She faced the stampeding cattle and spread her arms in front, fingers outstretched. Her fiery halo grew stronger until it seemed like leaping flames. The redness streamed from her fingertips towards the galloping cattle.

One by one they slowed down as they felt Lucy's awesome power tightening round them like an unseen rope. But there were too many of the creatures. Despite her power, Lucy was frightened.

The frenzied cows were all over the place. Lucy tried to send her gathering rays around them, casting the rays like a net. The distance was too great and the cattle too many. She began to feel her powers draining fast. The red glow started to flicker and fade. Her legs got wobbly and Lucy had to clutch at the statue with fumbling fingers to stop herself from falling. All at once Lucy knew she was going to faint.

An ear-splitting crack of thunder burst above her dizzy head and a bolt of lightning whammed down from the black sky. It struck Lucy from head to toe. The crowd fell back, half-blinded

by the intense glare. There was a hissing, sizzling noise and a crack split the statue in two, but it didn't collapse. Lucy stood transfixed by the lightning – it was a sight that everybody remembered for years afterwards. She glowed the most radiant red ever. Great cascades of shimmering sparks leapt from both Lucy and the statue.

The lightning died and Lucy zoomed into the air leaving a trail of glorious sparks behind. She dived and climbed and swooped between lamp-posts, rounding up the cattle and bringing them into a huddle round the smoking statue. Then with a broad grin on her smudgy face, she drove the timid beasts back down the High Street and into the market, to be sorted out by the farmers. The cattle behaved like little lambs. Only then did Lucy idly fly back to her parents and Nicholas.

'I could do with a cup of tea,' she said, wiping the hair from her eyes.

But the town would not let Lucy have a cup of tea. The whole family was surrounded by cheering shopkeepers and shoppers. They all wished to thank Lucy for saving the town from further damage. One man pushed his way to the front of the crowd. It was the travel agent.

'Is this your daughter?' he shouted at Mr and Mrs King. 'She was fantastic – and that lightning! It was incredible. I've never seen anything like it in my life. Lightning Lucy – that's what we ought to call her. Do you know Lightning Lucy just made two cows leave my shop? I thought they were going to eat all my aeroplane tickets.' He turned excitedly to Mr King. 'She saved my shop you know. I'm really very grateful. Look, about that deposit. Forget about it please. Just go ahead as planned.' Mr King looked at the travel agent with open mouth.

'What do you mean?' he stammered.

'Take the holiday!' cried the travel agent. 'Just go ahead as planned. How long were you going for?'

'Two weeks,' answered Mr King, in quite a daze.

'Make it four!' cried the travel agent happily. 'Don't worry about a thing. Your daughter has saved me far more than a holiday will cost.'

And so it was. Two months later, the King family were sitting on an aeroplane, flying to Greece, on a four week holiday.

'I still find it hard to believe,' said Mr King.

'Lightning Lucy,' murmured Mrs King. 'It's a good name. She's just like a thunder-storm at home, what with her noise and mess and everything.'

'Let's just hope there are no thunder-storms in Greece,' grinned Mr King. He glanced at

Lucy and Nicholas.

Nicholas was sitting back, staring out of the window and thoroughly enjoying his first flight. Leaning against his shoulder was his sister, fast asleep. Flying was nothing new to Lightning Lucy.

The Desperate Adventures of Sir Rupert and Rosie Gusset

by Jeremy Strong

'It's so exciting!' Rosie cried. 'Just think, Father, all those adventures! Fighting Mad Mavis! Looking for treasure!'

Just the thought of setting sail makes Sir Rupert feel seasick. And the possibility of bumping into his rival, Sir Sidney Dribble, or Mad Mavis and her pirate gang, makes him feel even worse. Luckily Sir Rupert's daughter, Rosie, isn't quite such a wimp as he is.

Fatbag the Demon Vacuum Cleaner

by Jeremy Strong

Elsie Bunce could see that Fatbag was no ordinary vacuum cleaner. He had a hungry-looking mouth and he seemed to be staring at her. But she didn't know that Fatbag was a Hoover with an evil plan!

READ MORE IN PUFFIN

Indoor Pirates on Treasure Island

by Jeremy Strong

Another hopelessly silly piratical adventure

Captain Blackpatch has always hated the sea – even though he's a pirate. His dastardly crew – Lumpy Lawson, Bald Ben and the twins Molly and Polly – don't like getting wet, and they all hate boats. So it's a pity that, when the pirates go camping, they get the idea that there's buried treasure on an island in the middle of a nearby lake. How can they reach it when they don't like water? Luckily Captain Blackpatch has a plan ...

The Karate Princess

by Jeremy Strong

Belinda, the youngest of sixteen, but by no means the prettiest, is not an ordinary princess. Can she win a handsome prince? Will she even want to? This is a fairy-tale with a twist - and a few kicks, punches and well-aimed blows to boot!

The Karate Princess to the Rescue

by Jeremy Strong

When Princess Belinda rushes off to rescue her karate teacher, held captive by the evil warlord Utagawa, she runs into trouble. Utagawa has the most powerful army of sumo wrestlers in the whole of Japan. Belinda's very best karate fails to defeat them. They are as big and powerful as elephants! Is there any other way to topple the super-strong sumos, or is the famous Karate Princess finally in for the chop?

READ MORE IN PUFFIN

There's a Pharoah in Our Bath!

by Jeremy Strong

A 4,000-year-old Pharaoh has come to stay . . .

It all starts when Carrie and Ben's dad brings home a mysterious man dressed from head to toe in rather stinky bandages. He turns out to be an ancient Egyptian Pharaoh called Sennapod. But Sennapod (Lord of Serpents, Master of Hippos) is on the run from two dastardly grave robber who are after his treasure.

Can Carrie and Ben help? And who on earth is Crusher of Worms?

READ MORE IN PUFFIN

There's a Viking in My Bed

by Jeremy Strong

Sigurd the Viking appears brandishing his sword Nosepicker. Mrs Tibblethwaite, a guest at the small seaside hotel, screams and Mr Ellis, the owner, drops down in a dead faint. What is a Viking doing in the twentieth century? And how will he be able to cope with his new life – with cars and washing-machines? And as for having a bath – what do you do with the soap if you're a Viking warrior?

The Fantora Family Files

by Adèle Geras

Ozymandias, the Keeper of the Files and guardian of the Family History, is a rather superior and gifted cat. In fact all the members of the Fantora family have special and unusual talents. Grandmother Filomena can predict the future, Eddie can grow anything, Rosie can concoct magic potions, while Auntie Varvara is a vegetarian vampire in search of Romance. The children, Bianca, Marco and Francesca, also have strange powers, which they use with hilarious and very unexpected results.

'A truly original, funny book'
– *Sunday Times*

My Best Fiend

by Sheila Lavelle

Angela is Charlie's best friend, or best fiend as Charlie accidently wrote in herschool essay. But fiend is probably a better word, as it's Angela's so-called marvellous ideas that always get Charlie into trouble. Like putting a spider in Miss McKenzie's sandwich, and plastering glue all over Laurence Parker's chair, and most fiendish of all, setting fire to her father's garage...

Friend or fiend, life is never dull for Charlie with Angela around in this, the first book of the hilarious and very popular fiend series.

Pongwiffy

by Kaye Umansky

Pongwiffy is a very smelly witch of *very* dirty habits. But she is a happy witch – until a gruesome gang of goblins move in next door and make her life miserable. So she asks her not-so-best friend Sharkadder to help her find a new slum and to advertise for a much-needed familiar. The trouble is, the only reply Pongwiffy gets is from a hamster! How *will* she explain this to the Witches' Covern?

A fantastically funny PONGWIFFY story!

READ MORE IN PUFFIN

For children of all ages, Puffin represents quality and variety – the very best in publishing today around the world.

For complete information about books available from Puffin – and Penguin – and how to order them, contact us at the appropriate address below. Please note that for copyright reasons the selection of books varies from country to country.

On the worldwide web: www.puffin.co.uk

In the United Kingdom: Please write to *Dept. EP, Penguin Books Ltd, Bath Road, Harmondsworth, West Drayton, Middlesex UB7 ODA*

In the United States: Please write to *Consumer Sales, Penguin USA, P.O. Box 999, Dept. 17109, Bergenfield, New Jersey 07621-0120.* VISA and MasterCard holders call 1-800-253-6476 to order Penguin titles

In Canada: Please write to *Penguin Books Canada Ltd, 10 Alcorn Avenue, Suite 300, Toronto, Ontario M4V 3B2*

In Australia: Please write to *Penguin Books Australia Ltd, P.O. Box 257, Ringwood, Victoria 3134*

In New Zealand: Please write to *Penguin Books (NZ) Ltd, Private Bag 102902, North Shore Mail Centre, Auckland 10*

In India: Please write to *Penguin Books India Pvt Ltd, 706 Eros Apartments, 56 Nehru Place, New Delhi 110 019*

In the Netherlands: Please write to *Penguin Books Netherlands bv, Postbus 3507, NL-1001 AH Amsterdam*

In Germany: Please write to *Penguin Books Deutschland GmbH, Metzlerstrasse 26, 60594 Frankfurt am Main*

In Spain: Please write to *Penguin Books S. A., Bravo Murillo 19, 1° B, 28015 Madrid*

In Italy: Please write to *Penguin Italia s.r.l., Via Felice Casati 20, I 20124 Milano.*

In France: Please write to *Penguin France S. A., 17 rue Lejeune, F-31000 Toulouse*

In Japan: Please write to *Penguin Books Japan, Ishikiribashi Building, 2–5–4, Suido, Bunkyo-ku, Tokyo 112*

In South Africa: Please write to *Longman Penguin Southern Africa (Pty) Ltd, Private Bag X08, Bertsham 2013*